W9-CCN-620

DATE DUE

Doctor Dolittle
Meets
the Pushmi-Pullyu

A DOCTOR DOLITTLE CHAPTER BOOK

Doctor Dolittle Meets the Pushmi-Pullyu

Text and pictures based on
The Story of Doctor Dolittle by Hugh Lofting

Adapted for Young Readers by N. H. Kleinbaum
Illustrated by Robin Preiss Glasser

A Yearling Book

Published by
Bantam Doubleday Dell Books for Young Readers
a division of
Random House, Inc.
1540 Broadway
New York, New York 10036

Library of Congress Cataloging-in-Publication Data

Kleinbaum, N. H.
    Doctor Dolittle meets the pushmi-pullyu : text and pictures based on The story of Doctor Dolittle by Hugh Lofting / adapted for younger readers by N. H. Kleinbaum ; illustrated by Robin Preiss Glasser.
        p.   cm.
    "A Doctor Dolittle chapter book."
    "A Yearling book."
    Summary: Doctor Dolittle travels to Africa to save the sick monkeys, and there he encounters the rarest of all animals, the pushmi-pullyu.
    ISBN 0-440-41550-0
    [1. Animals—Fiction. 2. Fantasy.] I. Lofting, Hugh, 1886–1947. Story of Doctor Dolittle. II. Glasser, Robin Preiss, ill. III. Title.
PZ7.K678354Dq   1999
[Fic]—dc21   98-32228
                                                                                   CIP
                                                                                    AC

Visit us on the Web! www.randomhouse.com
Educators and librarians, for a variety of teaching tools, visit us at
www.randomhouse.com/teachers

Book design by Patrice Sheridan
Printed in the United States of America
August 1999
10   9   8   7   6   5   4   3   2   1

Doctor Dolittle
Meets
the Pushmi-Pullyu

Chapter One

Chee-Chee, the Monkey

Once upon a time, there was a doctor named John Dolittle. He lived in a little town called Puddleby-on-the-Marsh.

Doctor Dolittle had a small house with a large garden. He loved animals, and he had many kinds of pets.

He had goldfish, rabbits, and white mice.

He had a squirrel, a hedgehog, a cow, a calf, and an old horse.

He even had a pet crocodile. The crocodile slept in the pond in the Doctor's gar-

den. The Doctor fed him well, so the crocodile didn't eat the fish in the pond.

But the Doctor's favorite pets were Dab-Dab, the duck; Jip, the dog; Gub-Gub, the baby pig; Polynesia, the parrot; and Too-Too, the owl.

Doctor Dolittle was a regular doctor who also treated animals.

Old ladies brought their dogs and cats to him. Farmers brought their sick cows and sheep and horses who had trouble seeing clearly.

The animals told the Doctor what was wrong with them. Then he cured them.

Soon animals all around the world knew that Dr. Dolittle could speak their language.

One day a new animal joined the Doctor's family.

Doctor Dolittle was sitting on his garden wall when an organ-grinder came by.

The organ-grinder had a monkey tied to a string.

The monkey looked very unhappy. The collar around his neck was too tight.

Doctor Dolittle took the monkey from the man. He gave the man a shilling and told him to go away.

The monkey stayed with Doctor Dolittle. The other animals named him Chee-Chee.

A Voyage

One night in December the Doctor and all his animals sat around the warm kitchen fire.

The Doctor read aloud from his books in animal language.

Suddenly the door flew open and Chee-Chee ran into the house.

"I have a message from my cousin in Africa!" he cried. "Hundreds of monkeys there are very sick. They beg you to come to Africa to help!"

"Who brought the message?" asked the Doctor.

"A swallow," Chee-Chee answered. "She is outside."

"Bring her in by the fire," said the Doctor.

The frightened swallow came in. She sat by the fire to get warm.

Then she told the Doctor all about the sick monkeys in Africa.

"I will go to Africa to help the monkeys," the Doctor said. "I will bring Chee-Chee, Polynesia, Jip, Dab-Dab, Gub-Gub, Too-Too, and the crocodile with me."

The monkey, the parrot, and the crocodile were very happy. They were going back to their real home!

The Doctor borrowed a ship from a friend who was a sailor.

Polynesia had been on long sea voyages before. She told the Doctor what they would need on the ship. They would have to buy a lot of food.

But Doctor Dolittle didn't have any money.

"Money is such a bother!" he sighed.

Doctor Dolittle was glad when the grocer said he could pay him back for the food after he returned from Africa.

The animals all helped pack for the trip.

Then they carried everything to the shore and loaded the ship.

They were ready to start the journey.

The swallow had been to Africa many times. She said she would lead the way.

The Doctor told Chee-Chee to pull up the ship's anchor.

The voyage began!

Shipwreck!

They sailed for six weeks.

As they sailed farther south it became warmer. Polynesia, Chee-Chee, and the crocodile loved the hot sun.

But the pig, dog, and owl did not like the hot weather at all.

They sat in the shade, drinking lemonade.

One evening Doctor Dolittle asked Chee-Chee to get the telescope.

"Soon we should see the shores of Africa," the Doctor said.

It grew darker and darker.

Suddenly a great storm hit. Thunder and lightning crashed. The wind howled. Rain poured down. High waves splashed right over the boat.

Then they heard a big BANG! The ship stopped and rolled on its side.

"What happened?" the Doctor asked Polynesia.

"I think we're shipwrecked," said the parrot. "Tell the duck to get out and see."

Dab-Dab dove into the waves.

When she came back, she said the ship had hit a rock. There was a big hole in the bottom of the boat. Water was coming in, and the ship was sinking fast.

"We must have run into Africa," the

Doctor said. "We'll all have to swim to land."

But Chee-Chee and Gub-Gub did not know how to swim!

"Get the rope," Polynesia called.

Dab-Dab took one end of the rope and flew to shore. She tied the rope to a palm tree. The Doctor tied the other end of the rope to the ship.

They all made it safely to the shore. Some of them swam. Some of them flew. Chee-Chee and Gub-Gub climbed along the rope to the land. They carried the Doctor's trunk and bag.

The rough sea beat the ship to pieces. They watched sadly as pieces of the ship floated away.

But they had made it safely to Africa.

The Doctor and his animals found shelter for the night in a dry cave in the cliffs.

Chapter Four

The Bridge of Apes

The next morning was bright and sunny.

Doctor Dolittle and the animals went down to the beach.

"Chee-Chee, do you know how to find the Land of the Monkeys?" the Doctor asked. "The sick monkeys are waiting for us."

Chee-Chee knew all the paths through the jungle. He led them through the trees to the Land of the Monkeys.

It was a long way, and they got very tired.

13

Finally they came to a steep cliff. A river
flowed below.

On the other side of the river was the
Land of the Monkeys.

The Doctor and his animals were worried. There was no way to get across.

But the monkeys on the other side began to make a bridge! They stretched across the river, holding each other's hands and feet.

The Doctor and his animals hurried across the bridge made of monkeys.

They all made it safely to the other side.

"You are the first human to see the famous Bridge of Apes," Chee-Chee told the Doctor.

Doctor Dolittle smiled. He was very pleased.

Chapter Five

The Leader of the Lions

As soon as they arrived at the monkeys' village, Doctor Dolittle was very busy.

Thousands of monkeys were sick.

The Doctor asked for the lions, leopards, and antelopes to come. He needed help taking care of the sick monkeys.

But the Leader of the Lions did not want to help.

"I am the King of Beasts! I will not wait on a lot of dirty monkeys!" he roared at Doctor Dolittle.

The lion was very angry. The Doctor tried hard not to look afraid.

"The monkeys are *not* dirty. They all had

a bath this morning," the Doctor said. "What if the lions get sick? If you don't help the monkeys, they might not help you when you are in trouble."

But the Leader of the Lions turned around and left.

The leopards and the antelopes also said they wouldn't help. They all left too.

Doctor Dolittle was very upset. Where could he get help to care for thousands of sick monkeys?

The Leader of the Lions went back to his den.

His wife, the Queen Lioness, was crying.

"One of the cubs is sick!" she said.

The Leader went and looked at his children. The two sweet little cubs lay on the floor. One did look very sick.

He returned to his wife. He proudly told her what he had said to the Doctor.

She was very angry.

"Go back right now!" she yelled. "Tell him you're sorry. Do *everything* the Doctor tells you. Maybe he will be kind enough to come and cure our cub."

So the Leader of the Lions went back to the Doctor.

"Do you have any help yet?" he asked.

"No," said the Doctor. "I'm very worried."

"I'll do what I can to help," the lion said. "I've told the other animals to come too. By the way, we have a sick cub at home. My wife is a little scared. Would you mind taking a look at him?"

"Of course I wouldn't," said the Doctor. He sighed with relief.

Soon animals from the forests, mountains, and plains came to help.

The monkeys began to get better.

Soon all the monkeys were well.

The Doctor's work was done. He was very tired.

He went inside his hut and slept for three days.

Chapter Six

The Pushmi-Pullyu

After he rested, the Doctor told the monkeys that he had to go back to Puddleby.

They were surprised and sad. They had hoped the Doctor would stay forever.

"Why is the good man going away?" the Chief Chimpanzee asked. "Isn't he happy here?"

"The Doctor owes money for our food," Chee-Chee said. "He must go home and pay it back."

"What is *money*?" the monkeys asked.

Chee-Chee told them that in the Doc-

tor's country you couldn't get food or clothing or anything without money.

The monkeys sat silently. They were thinking hard.

At last the Biggest Baboon stood.

He said, "We cannot let the Doctor go without a special present."

All the monkeys agreed.

"If you really want to make the Doctor happy, give him a rare animal they do not have in the zoos," Chee-Chee said.

"What are zoos?" asked the monkeys.

Chee-Chee said zoos were places for people to come and look at animals in cages.

The monkeys were shocked!

"That sounds like a prison!" one said.

Chee-Chee told the monkeys that the Doctor would be kind to the animal they gave him.

The Major of the Marmosets said they should give Doctor Dolittle an iguana.

"They have one in the London Zoo," Chee-Chee said.

"Do they have an okapi?" asked another.

"Yes. There is one in Belgium," Chee-Chee said.

"What about a pushmi-pullyu?" someone called out.

"No," Chee-Chee said. "No one has *ever* seen a pushmi-pullyu. Let's give him that!"

Pushmi-pullyus are extinct. That means there aren't any alive anymore. But long ago, a few pushmi-pullyus lived in the jungles of Africa.

Pushmi-pullyus looked very strange. They had no tail. They had two heads with sharp horns, one head at each end of their body.

There were no pushmi-pullyus in zoos. No one had ever caught one!

A pushmi-pullyu always faced you. Only one half slept at a time. The other head would always stay awake, watching.

They were also very shy animals.

The monkeys set out to find a pushmi-pullyu for Doctor Dolittle.

After a while they saw strange footprints near the edge of the river.

They followed the footprints to a place where the grass was high and thick.

"He must be in there!" one of the monkeys whispered.

The monkeys joined hands. They made a big circle around the high grass.

The pushmi-pullyu heard them.

He tried to run away, but he couldn't.

He sat down and waited to see what the monkeys wanted.

A Gift from
the Monkeys

One of the monkeys stepped forward. "Would you go back to Puddleby with Doctor Dolittle?" he asked.

"Certainly not!" said the pushmi-pullyu. He shook both of his heads hard.

The monkeys told the pushmi-pullyu that he would not be locked up in a zoo.

They said that the Doctor would show him to children and people in other parts of the world.

Then they told him about the Doctor's money problems.

Finally the pushmi-pullyu agreed to meet
Doctor Dolittle.

Chee-Chee took him to the Doctor.

"What in the world is this?" the Doctor
asked.

"This is the rarest animal of the African jungles," Chee-Chee said proudly. "It is called a pushmi-pullyu. It's the only two-headed beast in the world!"

The Doctor looked at the animal with wonder. He had never seen a creature like it.

"The pushmi-pullyu is a gift from the monkeys," Chee-Chee told the Doctor. "People will pay to see him. Take him home and you will make lots of money."

The Doctor looked at the frightened animal.

"But I don't want any money," he said.

"Yes, you do," said Dab-Dab. "We owe the grocer in Puddleby, and we need to get a new boat."

"Well, I would like to have a new pet," said the Doctor. "But do you really want to go with me?" he asked the creature.

"Yes," said the pushmi-pullyu. He nodded both heads.

The pushmi-pullyu felt he could trust the

Doctor. "You have been so kind to the animals here. But if I do not like your country, will you send me back home?"

"Of course!" said the Doctor. "Excuse me for asking, but are you related to the deer family?"

"Yes," the pushmi-pullyu said. "I am related to the gazelles, and the chamois on my mother's side. My father's great-grandfather was the last of the unicorns."

"I notice that you talk with only one of your mouths," said Dab-Dab. "Can't the other head talk?"

"Oh, yes," the pushmi-pullyu replied. "But I keep the other mouth for eating. That way I can talk while I eat without being rude."

And that was how Doctor Dolittle met the pushmi-pullyu.

Chapter Eight

A Farewell Party

The monkeys gave a big party to say goodbye to the Doctor.

There were many good things to eat and drink.

After they ate, the Doctor stood up.

"I am very sad to leave your beautiful country," he said. "But I must go because I have things to do at home. I hope you will all live happily ever after."

The monkeys clapped their hands for a very long time.

The Grand Gorilla rolled a great rock to the head of the table.

"This stone will always mark the spot of our special dinner," he said.

To this day, the stone is in that spot.

• • •

The monkeys found a new ship for Doctor Dolittle.

It was waiting for him at the shore.

When he got to the beach, the Doctor and his animals said goodbye to the monkeys.

The Doctor also said goodbye to Chee-Chee, Polynesia, and the crocodile.

They were all staying in Africa, the land where they were born.

Doctor Dolittle, Dab-Dab, Gub-Gub, Jip, and Too-Too boarded their new ship.

They sailed away from Africa.

They were sad to say goodbye to their friends, both new and old.

But everyone was ready to get back home.

Chapter Nine

Travels in England

The journey home was long and tiring.

But soon they reached England. The Doctor couldn't wait to get back home.

Jip reminded him that they had to pay back the money he owed in Puddleby.

So the Doctor asked the pushmi-pullyu if he could put him in a wagon. Then people could pay money to come and look at him.

The pushmi-pullyu said that was fine.

They traveled throughout the land. They stopped at every county fair and circus they could find.

The Doctor hung a big sign on the wagon. The sign said: COME AND SEE THE MARVELOUS TWO-HEADED ANIMAL FROM THE JUNGLES OF AFRICA. ADMISSION: SIXPENCE.

The Doctor's other animals rested underneath the wagon.

Doctor Dolittle sat in front.

The Doctor took money and answered questions about the pushmi-pullyu.

Zookeepers and people from the circus also came to see the two-headed animal.

They begged the Doctor to sell them the strange creature. They offered him a lot of money.

But the Doctor always said no.

"The pushmi-pullyu is free to come and go just like you and me," he said.

At first the traveling was fun. The animals met new friends. Doctor Dolittle talked to a lot of people about his travels.

Thousands of people came to the wagon and paid to see the pushmi-pullyu.

The Doctor made a lot of money.

But after a few weeks, they were all tired of it.

It was time to go home.

Chapter Ten

Home at Last

Everyone was glad to be back in Pud-dleby-on-the-Marsh.

There was a lot of dust all over the house. Dab-Dab was ready to take over the housekeeping.

The Doctor paid the grocer back for all the food they had taken on their voyage.

Even after paying back this money, the Doctor *still* had money left.

He had so much money left over, he had to get three more money boxes!

But that didn't change his mind about money.

"Money is such a bother!" he said. "But it *is* better not to have to worry about it. Now we'll be fine for the winter ahead."

And soon the winter came again. Snow flew against the kitchen window.

The Doctor and his animals, including the pushmi-pullyu, sat around the big fire.

The Doctor read aloud from his books.

Sometimes they talked about their adventures in Africa.

They wondered how their friends in Africa were doing.

Far away in Africa, the monkeys chattered about Doctor Dolittle too.

"I wonder what the good man is doing now," the monkeys asked each other. "Do you think he will ever come back?"

Polynesia squawked from high in a tree, "I think he will. I guess he will. I hope he will!"

And then, from the black mud of the river, the crocodile grunted:

"I'm SURE he will! Go to sleep!"

About the Author

Hugh Lofting was born in Maidenhead, England, in 1886 and was educated at home with his brothers and sister until he was eight. He studied engineering in London and at the Massachusetts Institute of Technology. After his marriage in 1912 he settled in the United States.

During World War I he left his job as a civil engineer, was commissioned a lieutenant in the Irish Guards, and found that writing illustrated letters to his children eased the strain of war. "There seemed to be very little to write to youngsters from the front; the news was either too horrible or too dull.

One thing that kept forcing itself more and more upon my attention was the very considerable part the animals were playing in the war. That was the beginning of an idea: an eccentric country physician with a bent for natural history and a great love of pets. . . ."

These letters became *The Story of Doctor Dolittle*, published in 1920. Children all over the world have read this book and the eleven that followed, for they have been translated into almost every language. *The Voyages of Doctor Dolittle* won the Newbery Medal in 1923. Drawing from the twelve Doctor Dolittle volumes, Hugh Lofting's sister-in-law, Olga Fricker, later compiled *Doctor Dolittle: A Treasury*, which was published by Dell in 1986 as a Yearling Classic.

Hugh Lofting died in 1947 at his home in Topanga, California.

About the Illustrator

Robin Preiss Glasser has had two wonderful careers so far, one as a dancer with the Pennsylvania Ballet and another as a designer and illustrator. She has a Bachelor of Fine Arts degree from the Parsons School of Design. She has designed theater sets and costumes, play programs, and posters. She has illustrated eight children's books, including Judith Viorst's *Alexander, Who's Not (Do You Hear Me? I Mean It!) Going to Move* and *You Can't Take a Balloon into the Metropolitan Museum*. Robin Preiss Glasser lives in Newport Beach, California, and has two children, Sasha and Benjamin.